A Very Corona Christmas

#Santa Stays Home

This **Christmas**
everyone has to stay home...

even Santa.

Published in 2020 by Kelley Donner
www.KelleyDonner.com

Information provided in A Little Donnerwetter books is not
intended to provide medical advice. If you are concerned about
the health and well being of you or your child,
you should always consult an appropriate
health care professional.

By the way, everything in this story is purely fictitious,
including the letters from world leaders. None of this happened...
at least not to the best of my knowledge.

First Edition 2020
ISBN 978-1-7339595-5-1

To my own little elves
Jonas, Lukas, and Max:

Thank you for reminding me
that anything can be possible,
if you only believe...

All the elves were gathered in the main lodge at the North Pole village awaiting Santa's big announcement.

"What could it be?"

asked Evan, the youngest of the elves.

"I don't know," said Liam, Evan's older brother, "but Santa had us stop production in the workshop today."

"What do you mean, stop production?"

asked Evan concerned.

"It means that we are not making any more toys. We've never stopped production before."

Liam's sentence was interrupted by a loud commotion at the door. Santa entered the workshop and looked surprisingly glum.

"Elves! Elves! Elves! Quiet please."

He reached into his red jacket and pulled out a pile of very official looking letters.

Santa tugged at his long, white beard.
He opened one letter, paused, and began to read...

Dear Santa Claus,

I am writing to inform you that you will

not be allowed to enter my country this

Christmas. We are currently not admitting any

foreigners, whatsoever, in order to reduce

the amount of Coronavirus transmissions.

Please use our postal system to deliver gifts

as it is the *fastest in the entire world!*

Sincerely,

The President of the United States

Followed by another letter...

Dear Santa,

Unfortunately, this year due to the current Coronavirus pandemic, we must ask you to follow these rules:

1. You are not allowed to enter any house by way of doors or chimneys.
2. Please always keep a distance of 2 meters from any parent or child.
3. All gifts will need to be quarantined for at least 48 hours before delivery.

Keep Calm and Carry On!
Your majesty, *Elizabeth R*

The Queen of England.

And another. And another.
The elves looked at each other in disbelief.

"What are we going to do now?"
said Evan quietly to his brother looking for any ray of hope.

"I don't know," said Liam. **"It looks like**
Christmas has been CANCELLED!"

Santa folded the letters and put them back into his pocket.
Then, after a long sigh, he continued speaking.

"This is a first for all of us at the North Pole.
This pandemic has put us in a very bad predicament.

We are lucky here at the North Pole to be so isolated
that we do not even have one case of the coronavirus!

However, if I travel around the world
delivering our presents to all the boys and girls,
I could catch the virus
and that would be risky for all of us."

Santa sighed,
and looked wearily at his elves.

"Therefore, it is with a sad and heavy heart that I announce to you today..."

Santa paused, unsure if he really wanted to continue, and then reluctantly stated,

"There will be no Christmas this year!

You are all to stop work indefinitely until this pandemic is over."

The elves gazed at each other in disbelief.

"No Christmas?
No Christmas?"

they all shouted simultaneously.

"This is going to be the worst Christmas ever!"

said one.

"This is a catastrophe!"

said another.

The elves began to talk
among themselves,
while taking in Santa's words.

None of them knew what to do.
They had never been out of work before.
One by one, they sorrowfully left the lodge and returned home.

Liam and Evan went back to their elf hut to think.

Evan sat down at his desk. It was piled high with letters from little boys and girls all over the world who had sent their wishes to Santa. He pushed the letters to one side.

"No need for these,"
       he thought and felt about as sad as he had ever felt.

"I'll make you a cup of hot tea," said his brother.

And, other than a few chores around their huts,
Liam, Evan and the rest of the elves had nothing to make and
nothing to do. For the next few days, they just sat around feeling
hopeless.

They yearned for the life they used to have.
They missed the way things used to be.
They missed the Christmas spirit.

Things didn't change much until one day a letter on Evan's table caught his eye. He opened it up and began to read.
Then he opened another one.

He began reading letter after letter.

He read what all the children had written and his eyes filled with tears. All around the world, children were all saying the same things. They, too, missed the way things used to be.

Suddenly, Evan jumped up from the table.

He pushed a few of the letters into his pocket, pulled on his elf boots and ran out the door.

Liam grabbed his coat and ran after him.

"**Evan!**" he called, catching up to him.
"**Evan, what are you doing?**"

"I'm going to save Christmas,"

he said.

Evan continued running until he arrived at Santa's front door.
He pounded on the door as loudly as he could.

Santa opened the door dressed in red sweatpants
and wearing a festive apron.

"Santa! Santa! I need to talk to you." Evan demanded,
barging into Santa's kitchen.

"Calm down, little elf." Santa answered,
"I just learned how to make my own sourdough bread.
Would you like to try some?"

Evan looked strangely at Santa, closed the door behind him
and put his hands on his hips.

"This is no time to begin to learn to bake,"
Evan answered.

"I'm sorry, Evan, but as you heard,
Christmas is cancelled this year," said Santa.

Then he pulled a piece of bread from the loaf and popped it
into his mouth.

"I can't go out. I can't even leave the North Pole.
I must shelter in place."

Evan pulled out the letter from his pocket and handed it to Santa.
"The children of the world NEED you, Santa!"

Santa read the letter, peered down at Evan and began to grin.
"Evan and Liam, go round up the other elves.

**There is something
I need to say
at once!"**

When all the elves were gathered again in the main lodge,
Santa began to speak.

"My dear elves. Evan, our youngest elf,
has shown me a letter which has reminded me
of why we are all here.

Dear Santa,

My name is Madeline. I am 7 years old and live in Brookfield, New Jersey. This year has been very difficult for my family.

I was unable to see my friends for a long time, and my dad lost his job. He said we don't have enough money for presents this year and that we are not able to celebrate Christmas. I told my dad that Santa would never cancel Christmas. You wouldn't Santa, would you? After everything that has happened this year, my gift from you is the one thing I know I can count on.

You are the best, Santa!

I love you,

Madeline

My dear elves, Madeline is right.
    Families all over the world have had their lives
        turned upside down.

Children everywhere need this Christmas
    more than ever before!"

Santa eyes began to twinkle again,
he straightened his hat, and continued,

"We have a duty to the boys and girls of the world.
Children deserve Christmas!"

Then he pushed up his sleeves and continued,

"Elves, it is time to get busy.
Bob, get the production line going again.
Shannon, start shining up my sleigh.
Sally and Tom, I need a Santa suit that can bring me into
        the homes of millions of children safely.

You are my smartest elves!

It is time to get to work."

The elves were elated and ran as fast as they could
to their workshop.

Santa contacted all of the world leaders and told them of his plan.
The elves were given access to the latest technology science
had to offer.

They worked, and polished, built, and painted.
This year, Christmas was going to be historic.

By Christmas Eve, everything was ready.

As the snow began to fall,
Santa stepped out of his lodge in a brand new Santa suit.
He looked a little different this year,
but he was now safe and ready to go.

It was time for Christmas,
and nothing
was going to stop him from
making children
happy this year,

not even the

Coronavirus.

As Santa flew off in his sleigh, he could be heard saying.

"Merry Christmas everyone!

Merry Christmas to you all!"

Dear Reader,

This has been a tough year for all of us.

Here's wishing you

A very merry Christmas!

From my house to yours.

Stay Safe!

Kelley Donner

Made in the USA
Coppell, TX
31 October 2020